Lost in You... Forever

"In the shadows of history, two hearts collide—one hiding a secret, the other chasing the truth."

For all the lovers

those who found each other,

those who lost,

.....

and those still searching.

Chapter 1

The Stranger in the Frame

The Safdarjung Tomb looked hauntingly beautiful at sunset—golden light melting into the stone, shadows stretching long across the courtyard. Anaya adjusted her camera, fixing the angle.

"Delhi's Hidden Love Stories, Episode 5," she whispered into the mic. "Legend says this tomb has seen lovers sneak in at midnight, whispering promises only the wind remembers."

She panned the camera left—arching doorways, intricate carvings—until suddenly, a face flashed on-screen.

A boy, half-hidden behind a pillar. Watching.

Anaya froze, her heart slamming into her ribs. She turned—but there was no one there.

"Weird," she muttered. She rewound the footage. There he was. Tall, sharp jawline, dark eyes that seemed to see through the lens.

The camera glitched.

And just like that—he was gone.

Next evening.

She had to find him. Maybe a history student? A local photographer? Whoever he was, he had aura—the kind that made her fingers itch to hit 'record.'

She returned to the tomb, camera in hand. Tourists shuffled around, but her eyes scanned the pillars, the archways, the silent corridors.

Nothing.

And then—

There.

He was sitting on the far steps, head bent over a sketchbook, pencil gliding over the page.

Anaya took a step closer, heart hammering.

"Hey!" she called.

He didn't look up.

Another step. "I saw you yesterday. In my camera."

This time, he paused—pencil mid-air. Slowly, he turned.

Up close, he was even more unsettling. Tousled hair, dark brows, and eyes that held secrets like locked doors.

He studied her, gaze flicking to her camera.

"Delete it."

Anaya blinked. "What?"

"The footage. Delete it." His voice was low, measured.

She smirked. "Wow. No 'hi, hello, nice to meet you'? Just straight to the drama?"

He held her stare. "Some stories shouldn't be told."

Anaya's fingers curled around her tripod. Intriguing.

"Too bad," she said, lifting her camera. "I like telling stories."

For the first time, he smiled—just a flicker, just enough to make her stomach tighten.

"Then you should be careful," he murmured.

"Why?"

His smirk deepened. "Because some stories bite back."

And before she could respond, he snapped his sketchbook shut— and walked away.

Leaving Anaya standing there, breathless… and hooked.

Chapter 2

The Boy Who Vanishes

Anaya watched him go, heart racing.

She had met plenty of guys—sweet, funny, overconfident—but none like him. There was something offbeat, something that made her pulse jump between fear and fascination.

Delete the footage?
Yeah, right.

She tightened her grip on her camera and scrolled through the clips. He was there. Crystal clear. But the moment she paused—

Glitch.

Her screen flickered, and his face blurred.

"What the hell?" she muttered.

She tried again. The moment the clip reached his frame—static. Like her camera was resisting.

Her fingers hesitated over 'Delete.'

Then she shook her head. No way.

The next day.

Zoya slurped her iced coffee obnoxiously. "So, let me get this straight. You saw a hot mystery boy—who told you to delete a video—so obviously, you're now obsessed?"

Anaya rolled her eyes. "Not obsessed. Just… curious."

Zoya smirked. "That's literally step one of obsession."

They were at a café near Lodhi Road, but Anaya's mind was still in Safdarjung Tomb.

Who was he? Why was he hiding?

"I have to find him again," she said.

Zoya arched a brow. "So we're stalking now? Love that for you."

Anaya ignored her, tapping her phone. "I'll start with social media. Someone in Delhi's art scene must know him. He was sketching something—maybe an architecture student?"

Zoya leaned forward. "Or a ghost."

Anaya deadpanned. "Really?"

Zoya shrugged. "C'mon, disappearing act? Camera glitching? It's literally a horror movie setup."

Anaya shook her head. "He's real."

But as she scrolled through Instagram, typing keywords—Safdarjung sketches, Delhi artists, tomb painters—a strange chill ran down her spine.

Because no matter how much she searched, there was no sign of him.

Not a single photo, account, or tag.

As if he didn't exist at all.

Sunset. Safdarjung Tomb.

She returned. Alone.

The place was quieter, the air heavy with history. A few tourists lingered, but no sign of him.

Her camera was ready.

She scanned the pillars, the corridors, the steps—nothing.

"Okay, mystery boy," she muttered. "You wanted me to stay away? Too bad."

She raised her camera to film the sunset—

And there he was.

Sitting on the same steps.

Calm. Unbothered. As if he had been there the whole time.

Her breath hitched. "You again."

He didn't even turn. "You again."

She walked over, crossing her arms. "Funny, I looked for you online. You don't exist."

Now he glanced up, lips curving into that smirk.

"Maybe you searched in the wrong place."

Anaya narrowed her eyes. "And where should I be looking?"

His gaze held hers. "Where they keep the stories that never got written."

Something in his voice sent a shiver down her spine.

But before she could press him—before she could ask his name—

A group of tourists walked past.

And in that single second of distraction—

He was gone.

Like a ghost.

Like he had never been there at all.

Chapter 3

DM Slips & Hidden Clues

Anaya rushed to the spot where he had been sitting.
Empty.
No footsteps, no trace—nothing.

She turned in circles, scanning the tomb's courtyard. How did he
disappear so fast?

A few tourists stared as she muttered to herself, but she didn't care.
This wasn't normal.

And she hated not knowing.

Midnight. Anaya's Room.

Anaya lay on her bed, staring at her laptop. Tabs were open—Delhi art forums, local university sketch clubs, Instagram deep dives—but all she had were dead ends.

The guy was nowhere online.

She sighed, unlocking her phone. Maybe it was just—

PING.

A DM notification.

Unknown User: "Stop chasing ghosts, Anaya."

Her stomach flipped.

She bolted upright.
Who the hell—?

She clicked the profile. No picture. No bio. No posts.

Just a username: @R_Vanishes.

She swallowed. R.

Could it be—?

Her fingers hovered over the keyboard. Then she typed back.

Anaya: "Who are you?"

The reply came instantly.

@R_Vanishes: "The real question is—who are you looking for?"

Anaya's heartbeat slammed in her chest.

Okay. Creepy.

She exhaled, steadying herself.
If this was some internet prank—she wasn't playing along.

Anaya: "You're the guy from Safdarjung, aren't you?"

Silence. No reply.

Seconds passed. Then a new message popped up.

@R_Vanishes: "Some things are better left unseen."

And just like that—

The account disappeared.

Vanished.

Like it had never existed at all.

Chapter 4

Midnight Dare at the Tomb

"You're actually going back?" Zoya's voice crackled over the phone.

Anaya zipped up her hoodie, checking her camera battery. Full charge. Good.

"I have to," she said.

It had been three days since the DM. Three days of no replies, no sign of him. @R_Vanishes was gone.

But her gut told her—this wasn't over.

Safdarjung Tomb at night? Risky. But worth it.

Zoya sighed. "At least take a weapon."

Anaya smirked. "I have my camera."

"Oh wow. Gonna record your own kidnapping? Genius."

"Relax. If I die, you get my Spotify playlist."

Zoya groaned. "You're impossible."

But Anaya was already out the door.

Midnight. Safdarjung Tomb.

The streets were empty, the tomb's iron gates locked.

But Anaya knew a side entrance. She had filmed here enough times to know the blind spots.

With her hoodie pulled low, she slipped through the broken fence.

Inside, the air was thicker. The tomb stood like a silent guardian of forgotten stories.

She pressed record.

"Midnight at Safdarjung. If Delhi has a heart, this is where it beats the loudest—where the past whispers and the present listens."

Her own voice echoed, and for a second, she felt stupid. What was she even expecting?

And then—she heard it.

A soft sound. Footsteps.

Her breath caught.

She swung the camera toward the arches. The shadows flickered— and there he was.

Standing at the far end of the corridor. Watching her.

Anaya's pulse spiked.

She lifted her camera.

"Hey!" she called.

He didn't move.

"Who are you?"

Silence.

She stepped forward. "Why do you keep disappearing?"

This time, he spoke. His voice was calm, almost amused.

"You shouldn't be here."

Anaya's grip tightened. "Neither should you."

A smirk. "You broke in."

"So did you."

His eyes held hers for a long second. Something unreadable. Something dangerous.

And then—he turned. Walking away.

"Wait!" Anaya rushed after him. "I have questions!"

But as she turned the corner—

He was gone.

Again.

But this time—

He had left something behind.

A scrap of paper. Folded. Stuffed into the cracks of the stone wall.

Anaya's fingers trembled as she picked it up. Unfolded it.

A sketch.

Of her.

Sitting right there, camera in hand.

Drawn days before she had even met him.

Her breath hitched.

The inked words below made her skin prickle.

"You're getting too close, Anaya."

Chapter 5

The Name in the Archives

Anaya stared at the sketch.

Her face, her posture—exactly how she had been sitting two nights ago.

But the problem was... this was drawn before she even met him.

Her fingers tightened around the paper.

Who was he? And how did he know her before she even found him?

Next Morning. Delhi University Library.

Zoya tapped her nails against the table. "So, let me get this straight—again."

Anaya shushed her. The archives section was nearly empty, dust hanging in the golden morning light.

"You think this guy is some kind of—what? A time traveler? A stalker artist?" Zoya whispered dramatically.

Anaya ignored her, flipping through an old book on Safdarjung Tomb's history. "There has to be something. Some connection."

Zoya sighed, stuffing a samosa into her mouth. "And how do you know he's even real? Maybe you're hallucinating. Maybe you need more sleep."

Anaya stiffened.

Because just then—she found it.

A black-and-white photograph.

The Safdarjung Tomb, dated 1942.

And in the background—under an archway—

A boy.

Standing exactly where he had been standing last night.

The same pose. The same sharp features.

Zoya choked on her samosa. "What the actual—?!"

Anaya's throat went dry.

She flipped the page, looking for more information.

And then she saw it—his name.

"Rehan Safvi. 1923-1947."

Zoya grabbed her wrist. "Hold up. If this photo is from the 1940s and this guy looks exactly like your mystery boy—"

Her voice lowered.

"Anaya... he's dead."

A chill ran down Anaya's spine.

She glanced at the sketch in her hand.

The message written in ink.

"You're getting too close, Anaya."

Her heartbeat slammed in her chest.

Too close to what?

Chapter 6

The Secret Beneath the Tomb

Anaya couldn't breathe.

Rehan Safvi. 1923-1947.

Dead. For over 75 years.

Yet she had met him. Spoke to him. Chased him through the tomb.

Zoya was pale. "Tell me you're not thinking what I think you're thinking."

Anaya looked at the old photograph again. Rehan's eyes. Even in black and white, they held that same knowing smirk.

"There's only one way to find out."

Zoya groaned. "Let me guess—you're going back?"

Anaya shoved the book into her bag. "And this time, I'm not leaving without answers."

Midnight. Safdarjung Tomb.

The air was heavier tonight.

Anaya climbed over the broken fence, her breath misting in the cold. No tourists, no guards. Just the whisper of the past pressing against her skin.

She walked slowly to the same spot. The archway where she had seen him—where he had disappeared.

"Rehan." Her voice barely echoed.

Silence.

Her fingers tightened around the sketch. "I know who you are."

Still, nothing.

She exhaled. Think, Anaya. If he wasn't here, where—

Her gaze snapped downward.

The old stone floor. Slightly uneven.

She knelt, tracing the cracks with her fingertips. Some of the slabs looked... different.

A trapdoor?

Her heart pounded. She pulled out a pocket knife and wedged it between the cracks.

A sharp creak.

The slab shifted.

Anaya stumbled back as a hidden wooden staircase revealed itself— leading underground.

Her breath hitched. What the hell?

She pulled out her phone, turning on the flashlight.

The stairs descended into darkness.

A rational part of her brain screamed—don't go in.

But the other part? The part that had seen a dead boy's face in a 1942 photograph?

It was already stepping down.

One slow step at a time.

Chapter 7

The Room That Time Forgot

Anaya stepped deeper into the darkness.

The air was thick, stale—like it had been trapped for decades. Her phone flashlight barely cut through the blackness as the stairs twisted downwards.

Every step creaked under her weight.

And then—she reached the bottom.

A long, narrow hallway stretched ahead.

Old, damp stone walls. A scent of earth and forgotten time.

Anaya swallowed. Who built this? And why?

She moved forward, trailing her fingers along the wall—until they hit something cold.

Metal. A door.

A rusted, ancient iron door, half buried under dust.

Her breath caught.

Faint scratches marked its surface, as if someone had tried to claw their way out.

A chill ran down her spine.

She gripped the handle. Turned.

The door groaned, resisting at first—then swung open.

And inside—

Anaya froze.

A Room That Shouldn't Exist.

The air shifted. It wasn't just a room. It was a study.

A desk covered in ink bottles. Stacks of half-finished sketches.

A massive, ornate mirror covered in dust.

And on the walls—

Anaya's stomach flipped.

Because they were covered in portraits of her.

Dozens.

Sketches, paintings, even old photographs.

But how?

Some were from last week, the exact moment she had sat by the tomb.

Some were from years ago—a photo of her as a child, holding her father's hand at India Gate.

And then—a drawing of her she had never seen before.

Older. In her twenties. Looking back at the very mirror in this room.

Anaya staggered back.

"This isn't possible."

Her pulse hammered.

And then—she saw it.

The desk drawer. Slightly open.

She stepped forward, hands trembling.

Pulled it open.

Inside, there was just one thing.

A folded paper.

Anaya slowly unfolded it.

Her own handwriting stared back at her.

"Anaya, if you're reading this—stop. Get out. Before it's too late."

Her breath hitched.

A footstep sounded behind her.

She spun around.

And standing in the doorway—

Was Rehan.

Watching her.

With a look that wasn't quite human anymore.

Chapter 8

The Mirror That Sees Everything

Rehan stood in the doorway.

Silent. Still. His dark eyes locked onto hers.

Anaya's pulse raced. Her mind screamed: Run. But her feet refused to move.

He took a slow step forward. No shadow stretched behind him.

"Did you draw these?" Her voice barely came out.

A pause. Then, softly—

"I didn't have a choice."

Anaya's fingers tightened around the letter.

"What does that mean?"

His jaw tensed. "It means you shouldn't be here."

Her breath hitched. "Then why did you leave me clues? Why let me find this place?"

Rehan exhaled sharply. "Because... you were always meant to."

The air thickened.

Anaya's eyes flicked toward the massive mirror. It loomed over the room, coated in decades of dust.

Something about it felt wrong.

Rehan noticed her stare. His expression darkened.

"Don't," he warned.

But Anaya already moved.

She reached out—wiped the dust away.

And gasped.

The Mirror Showed Two Realities.

The reflection wasn't just hers.

It showed her and Rehan standing together—but in a different time.

A sepia-toned world, where Anaya wasn't wearing her hoodie, but an old-fashioned salwar kameez.

And Rehan…

Rehan looked alive.

No ghostly presence, no eerie silence—just a boy, laughing, his hand casually resting on her wrist.

Anaya's heart pounded.

"What is this?" she whispered.

Rehan's voice was quiet. Pained.

"It's… a door."

Her breath caught. "A door to where?"

He hesitated.

Then—

"To the life we never got."

The Truth Unfolds.

Anaya's stomach twisted.

"You're saying I—" She swallowed. "I was in that time? With you?"

Rehan held her gaze.

"Yes."

Something in her chest tightened.

Memories she didn't recognize stirred. A flash of laughter in the rain. Fingers brushing over ink-stained pages. A whispered promise beneath the same Safdarjung arch.

A life she never lived—yet somehow remembered.

"No," she murmured, shaking her head. "That's not possible."

Rehan stepped closer.

"You don't believe me?" His voice was low, almost desperate.

Anaya's throat felt dry. "I—"

And then—

The mirror shuddered.

A ripple ran across the glass, distorting their reflections.

And Anaya's own reflection—

Turned. To look directly at her.

She staggered back.

"What the hell—?"

The other Anaya smiled. Soft. Familiar. Haunting.

And then—

She reached out.

Straight through the glass.

A hand grabbed Anaya's wrist.

Cold. Too cold.

A voice whispered—

"It's time to come back."

And before Anaya could even scream—

The mirror shattered.

Chapter 9

Trapped Between Two Timelines

Glass exploded.

Anaya felt herself falling— but not onto cold stone.

Instead—

The air shifted.

The musty scent of the hidden room vanished. The darkness of the tomb faded.

And when Anaya opened her eyes—

She wasn't in 2025 anymore.

Delhi, 1945.

Sunlight warmed her skin.

The Safdarjung Tomb stood before her, but it wasn't abandoned and crumbling.

It was alive.

The marble gleamed, newly polished. The gardens were lush, untouched by time. People strolled past, dressed in pre-independence India's fashion. Men in Nehru jackets. Women in elegant sarees.

A hand tightened around hers.

Anaya spun around—

And there he was.

Rehan.

But this Rehan wasn't a ghost.

His eyes weren't haunted. His body wasn't a flicker of the past.

He was real. Warm. Alive.

"Anaya?" he murmured, brows furrowed.

Like she was the one who had changed.

Anaya's heart slammed in her chest.

This wasn't a dream.

She was here.

She was really here.

Memories That Don't Belong to Her.

Her breath came shaky. "Rehan, I—"

A rush of images flooded her mind.

A life she didn't remember—but somehow belonged to.

Sitting by the Yamuna River, sketching side by side.

Sneaking into old bookstores. Stealing glances over steaming chai.

A midnight promise in whispers: "We'll leave together. Find a future beyond this city."

Anaya stumbled back.

She knew these moments.

But they weren't hers.

They were this timeline's Anaya.

A girl who had loved Rehan before time had ripped them apart.

And now... she had taken her place.

No Way Back.

She turned wildly, searching for the mirror.

For anything that could pull her home.

But the mirror was gone.

The underground room, the hidden study—none of it had ever existed in this time.

Her pulse pounded.

She was stuck.

Rehan's grip on her wrist tightened. "Anaya, what's wrong? You look like you've seen a ghost."

A ghost.

The irony almost made her laugh.

She had spent so much time chasing Rehan's past—

And now, she was the one lost in it.

Chapter 10

Love That Defies Time

-"When fate offers a second chance, do you take it... or fight to return?"

Anaya's mind raced.

This wasn't just a dream. She was here.

Stuck in 1945.

Rehan was alive. His fingers were warm around her wrist, his eyes filled with concern.

She should have been terrified.

Instead, she felt something worse—

A pull.

A longing so deep, it made her question everything.

The World That Knew Her.

People passed by, nodding at her.

They recognized her.

A woman in a bright saree smiled. "Anaya beti, did you finish your new sketch?"

A shopkeeper called out, "Your father was looking for you, bibi. Said something about dinner at home."

Home.

She had a home here. A life.

But it wasn't hers.

Not really.

Her chest tightened. "Rehan… I don't belong here."

He laughed. "What do you mean? You've always belonged here."

No.

She belonged to a different Delhi. A Delhi with iPhones, metro stations, and Instagram reels.

Not this.

Not him.

And yet…

She couldn't let go.

The Promise of a Different Future.

Rehan pulled her toward the steps of the tomb.

"Come," he said, grinning. "I want to show you something."

She followed—because what else could she do?

He led her inside the tomb, past the grand pillars, up a narrow flight of stairs.

At the top, the whole city stretched beneath them.

"Beautiful, isn't it?" he murmured.

Anaya nodded, barely breathing.

"I always knew you'd leave one day," Rehan said softly. "You've always wanted more than this city could give you."

Anaya's throat tightened.

She had said those words.

Not her.

But the Anaya who belonged here.

The girl whose life she was now wearing like a stolen dress.

And suddenly—she knew.

If she didn't find a way back now…

She never would.

The Final Choice.

The sun was setting.

Anaya looked at Rehan, his eyes reflecting the orange glow.

Her heart ached.

Because for a moment—a small, dangerous moment—she wanted to stay.

To forget her real life. To be his Anaya.

To love him in a time that wasn't hers.

But she couldn't.

Her family, her world—they were waiting for her.

And if she didn't leave now, she never would.

She stepped back.

"I have to go."

Rehan frowned. "Go where?"

Anaya didn't answer.

Because she had no idea how.

Until—

A gust of wind whipped through the tomb.

And behind Rehan—the mirror reappeared.

The same ancient glass.

But this time—

It showed her real life.

Delhi in 2025.

A world waiting for her to step back in.

Her breath caught.

Rehan turned—saw it too.

His face darkened.

"You're leaving," he whispered.

Tears burned her eyes. "I have to."

Rehan exhaled shakily. "Will I ever see you again?"

She didn't know.

But she lied anyway.

"Yes."

He smiled—just a little.

And before she could change her mind—

She stepped into the mirror.

Epilogue

The Stranger in the Café

Delhi, 2025.

The coffee shop buzzed with quiet chatter, the scent of freshly brewed espresso lingering in the air.

Anaya sat by the window, fingers drumming against her cup. She had been searching for weeks.

Following every clue. Every name, every whisper, every feeling.

But Rehan was nowhere.

Had she imagined it all?

Had time played a cruel trick on her?

Maybe she was never meant to find him.

Maybe he had moved on.

Or worse—maybe he had never existed in this life.

She sighed, glancing out at the busy street.

And then—

A voice.

Low. Familiar. Too familiar.

"Is this seat taken?"

Anaya froze.

Slowly, she looked up.

And there he was.

Not in old-time clothes. Not a flickering ghost.

Just a guy.

In a black hoodie. A watch on his wrist. A tired but amused smile on his lips.

But his eyes—

They were the same.

Deep. Knowing. Rehan's eyes.

Anaya's heart slammed against her ribs.

He found me.

She couldn't breathe. Couldn't speak.

The moment stretched too long, too fragile.

And then—he smirked.

"Did you think I'd forget you so easily, Anaya?"

Her vision blurred. Tears. Laughter. Relief.

She shook her head.

And for the first time in weeks—

She knew.

Their love story wasn't over.

It had just begun.

The End.

Or maybe... just the beginning?